GOLDEN CHILD

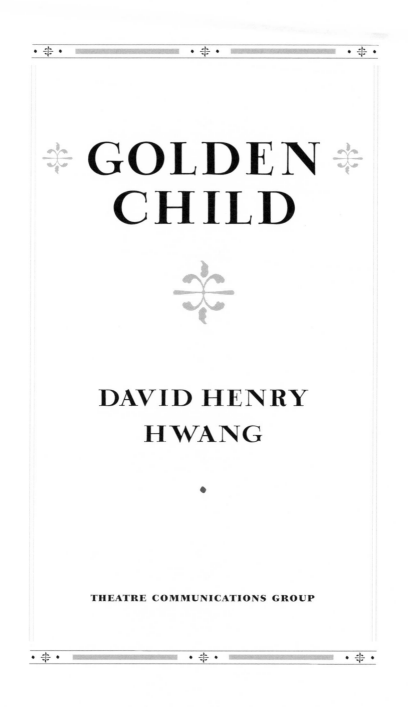

GOLDEN CHILD

DAVID HENRY HWANG

•

THEATRE COMMUNICATIONS GROUP

Golden Child is published by Theatre Communications Group, Inc.,
355 Lexington Ave., New York, NY 10017–0217.

This publication is made possible in part with public funds from
the New York State Council on the Arts, a State Agency.

Hwang, David Henry, 1957–
Golden Child / by David Henry Hwang. — 1st ed.
ISBN 1-55936-158-1
(pbk. : alk. paper)
1. Converts from Confucianism—China—Drama.
2. Family—China—Drama.
I. Title.
PS3558.W83 G65   1998
812'.54—dc21   98–49477
CIP

Book design and typography by Lisa Govan
Cover design by Lisa Govan
Cover art by Serino Coyne, Inc.

First Edition, December 1998

BRINGING UP "CHILD"

Each play defines its own journey toward completion. Some emerge relatively complete, needing only a few nips and tucks before going out to face the world. Some are problem children who, despite all efforts, never seem to find themselves. The Broadway opening of my most recent show, *Golden Child*, represents the culmination of an unusual voyage, one which began germinating thirty years ago in the mind of a ten-year-old child.

Golden Child is inspired by the story of my great-grandfather, who converted to Christianity in China around the turn of the century. The play reimagines the wrenching changes he set into motion, which forever changed the world of his three wives (Chinese society of that era was polygamous) and one of his daughters. That daughter is based on my maternal grandmother. Decades after the world of *Golden Child* had passed into history, when I was a ten-year-old American boy, that same grandmother fell gravely ill. I knew her as the only person of her generation who remembered our family history, and I feared that with her passing, the lore of our ancestors would be lost. As an American boy, growing up in Southern California, these stories somehow seemed very important to me, so I asked my parents if I could spend my summer vacation in the city of Cebu in the Philippines, where she was living at the time. They agreed, and I embarked with my "Ama" upon the collection of what we might now call oral histories. When I returned to Los Angeles, I compiled the tape-recorded information into a ninety-page "novel" on the history of my family, which I titled *Only Three Generations,* after the Chinese proverb: "The wealth of a Chinese family lasts only three generations." This document was duly Xeroxed and distributed to my relatives, who showered it with excellent reviews.

Almost three decades later, in early 1995, I returned to my manuscript as a middle-aged man, and began to collaborate with my ten-year-old self to create a new play. At ten, could I have known that my adult self would one day return to this work? Probably not. But something at that young age did compel me to record these stories, to ensure that my life as an American would exist in a context more real and human than the "Charlie Chans" or "Fu Manchus" I saw on television or in the movies.

My first draft of *Golden Child* was completed that June. Several months later, I heard the piece read for the first time at South Coast Repertory in Costa Mesa, California, which had commissioned the work. I learned that, though the germ of a good play lay somewhere within, the text was too wordy. Furthermore, its structure, which juxtaposed scenes of pre-Revolutionary China with monologues by a contemporary figure recounting memories of his grandmother, felt awkward and unwieldy. The impact of the Chinese scenes vastly outweighed that of the contemporary character's speeches.

In the summer of 1996, I workshopped *Golden Child* in Breadloaf, Vermont, the summer home of Providence's Trinity Repertory Company, where I am Artist-in-Residence under the Pew/TCG National Artist Residency Program. Working with actors (including Tsai Chin and Julyana Soelistyo, who have remained on this journey since its inception), I pared down the contemporary monologues and hacked away at the excess dialogue.

South Coast Repertory agreed to present *Golden Child* as a co-production with The Joseph Papp Public Theater/New York Shakespeare Festival, which had premiered my first four plays under the leadership of the late Joseph Papp. During rehearsals at the Public, in the fall of 1996, I came to rely on the unerring theatrical instincts of director James Lapine, a Tony Award- and Pulitzer Prize-winning author himself, who contributed ideas for some of the play's best moments, and whose notes, I conceded to my growing irritation, were almost always correct. We added scenes, turned the contemporary monologues into a framing device for the central historical story and continued to trim excess verbiage.

Golden Child opened at the Public to mixed-to-favorable reviews. Producer Benjamin Mordecai stepped in and encouraged us to continue working on the play, culling whatever we found useful from the notices, with an eye toward bringing the show to Broadway. For the play's next incarnation, again at South Coast Repertory, James and I turned the contemporary monologues into short bookend scenes and worked on replacing historical explanation with dramatic action. In search of these moments, I returned to my original text and came upon a scene involving my great-grandfather's decision to unbind my grandmother's feet, reversing a centuries-old tradition which had turned women into cripples in the name of feminine beauty. Such a moment had only been talked about but not dramatized in the Public production.

Suddenly, Tiong-Yee stomped over to his eldest daughter and ripped the bindings off her feet. His wife lowered her head and answered in as straight a tone as she could manage, "Don't you care about your daughters? Don't you want them to marry someday? No person of fine class would marry a girl whose feet are not bound. You must bind the feet of girls so that they will not grow, and they shall be pretty with their tiny new feet."

Tiong-Yee's rebuttal was strong: "This is a new century. These are new times. My daughters will be educated—they will go to school, learn to read and write, just like a man—maybe even go to college. I have seen many things in my trips over the seas. I have talked to and even made friends with these white Western people. The times are changing—even you will see one day. Is that clear?"

As a child, such courage on the part of my great-grand-father seemed natural and uncomplicated. As an adult, how-ever, I could not help but reflect upon the ambivalence he must have felt in breaking with tradition, knowing he was risking the future of his children, and would be criticized for his actions. In a beautiful sequence suggested by James, Tiong-Yee (renamed Tieng-Bin in the play) must struggle with his senior wife, and then with the ghosts of his own ancestors, in order to unbind the feet of his daughters.

At the play's next stop, Washington, D.C.'s Kennedy Center, we perhaps misstepped. The tone of *Golden Child* ranges from humorous to tragic. James had long stressed to me the importance of striking a balance in which the comedy does not compromise the show's more serious conclusion. I, however, had consistently pushed him to emphasize the laughs, and at this venue I got my wish. The result was too glib and shallow, our second-act tribulations unearned. Our producers decided to postpone our return to New York until the following season.

The entire time we worked on the play, I questioned whether I, an American, could authentically recreate the world of Old China. Several of my earlier works had been staged in the island republic of Singapore, one of the few places in Asia where an English-language work can reach a large native audience. I liked the idea of a Broadway-bound work trying-out in Asia rather than a more conventional American or English venue. In December 1997, we began rehearsals for a stop at the Singapore Repertory Theatre, the next leg on our final push toward Broadway. In the interim, I had rethought the character of the male patriarch as an older man, whose decision to change would be more difficult, and whose fall might carry greater weight. With this in mind, we recast several roles to assemble our Broadway-bound cast, which now included the great classical actor Randall Duk Kim, with whom I had wanted to work all my life.

We were received with great warmth and excitement in Singapore; literally not an empty seat was available for our entire run. As the child of immigrants, I felt a particular pride in the response of the Singaporean Chinese, many of whom told me that the work had caused them to rediscover their own ancestral histories. Whatever *Golden Child's* eventual fate back in the States, I knew I would always cherish the way this work had touched an audience in Asia. Still there was more work to be done. Returning to the American Conservatory Theatre in San Francisco, we continued to rework the framing scenes and clarify the male lead's reasons for converting to Christianity, as well as his relationships with his wives.

Looking back upon the twists and turns of this journey, I sometimes see it as an American playwright's act of ancestor worship. If we look at traditional ancestor worship from a psychological standpoint, we may regard it as self-exploration—the living inventing both sides of altar conversations to keep the dead alive. Undoubtedly, returning to this material allowed me to invent many sides of numerous conversations, and to remember my forebears the way I know best: upon the stage. I also agree, however, that plays are like children, which at some point must be let go to find their own way in the world. So with the premiere of *Golden Child*, I simultaneously claim and release my ancestors, until perhaps some future point when I may need to call upon them again, to travel together down another road.

David Henry Hwang
April 1998

GOLDEN CHILD

PRODUCTION HISTORY

Golden Child was commissioned by South Coast Repertory (David Emmes, Producing Artistic Director; Martin Benson, Artistic Director), Costa Mesa, California. It was first workshopped by Trinity Repertory Company in residence at the Breadloaf School of English, with assistance from the Pew/TCG National Artist Residency Program. The play premiered November 17, 1996, at The Joseph Papp Public Theater/New York Shakespeare Festival, George C. Wolfe, Producer. Sets were by Tony Straiges, lights by Richard Nelson and David J. Lander, costumes by Martin Pakledinaz and sound by Dan Moses Schreier. The production stage manager was Buzz Cohen. James Lapine directed the following cast:

ENG AHN
Julyana Soelistyo

ANDREW KWONG/ENG TIENG-BIN
Stan Egi

ELIZABETH KWONG/ENG ELING, THIRD WIFE
Liana Pai

ENG SIU-YONG, FIRST WIFE
Tsai Chin

ENG LUAN, SECOND WIFE
Jodi Long

REVEREND ANTHONY BAINES
John Christopher Jones

Golden Child was further developed in productions at South Coast Repertory; The John F. Kennedy Center for the Performing Arts/Eisenhower Theater (James A. Johnson, Chairman; Lawrence J. Wilker, President); The Singapore Repertory Theatre (Tony Petito, Artistic Director); and the American Conservatory Theatre (Carey Perloff, Artistic Director; Heather Kitchen, Managing Director). On April 2, 1998, *Golden Child* was presented at Broadway's Longacre Theatre by Benjamin Mordecai, Dori Berinstein, John Kao, Talia Shire Schwartzman and the above theatrical institutions. Sets were by Tony Straiges, lights by David J. Lander, costumes by Martin Pakledinaz and sound by Dan Moses Schreier. The production stage manager was Allison Sommers. James Lapine directed the following cast:

ENG AHN
Julyana Soelistyo

ANDREW KWONG/ENG TIENG-BIN
Randall Duk Kim

ELIZABETH KWONG/ENG ELING, THIRD WIFE
Ming-Na Wen

ENG SIU-YONG, FIRST WIFE
Tsai Chin

ENG LUAN, SECOND WIFE
Kim Miyori

REVEREND ANTHONY BAINES
John Horton

SERVANTS/GHOSTS
Julienne Hanzelka Kim, Lisa Li, James Saito

CHARACTERS

ENG AHN
Grandmother of Andrew Kwong,
daughter of Tieng-Bin and Siu-Yong

ANDREW KWONG/ENG TIENG-BIN
Husband of Elizabeth/Husband of Three Wives,
Ahn's father

ELIZABETH KWONG/ENG ELING, THIRD WIFE
Andrew's wife/Tieng-Bin's Third Wife

ENG SIU-YONG, FIRST WIFE
Tieng-Bin's First Wife

ENG LUAN, SECOND WIFE
Tieng-Bin's Second Wife

REVEREND BAINES
Friend of Tieng-Bin

PLACE

Manhattan and Eng Tieng-Bin's
home village near Amoy, in Southeast China

TIME

ACT ONE: The present and winter 1918
ACT TWO: Spring 1919 and the present

ACT ONE

Fade up on Ahn, a Chinese girl of ten, who speaks in the voice of an eighty-five-year-old woman.

AHN: Andrew—you must be born again.

> (*Lights up on Andrew Kwong, Asian, fifties, in bed beside Elizabeth—the same actress who will later play Eling. He sits up with a start, awakening her.*)

ELIZABETH: What?
ANDREW: Nothing.
AHN: Make money, not important; write successful book, not important. Only one thing important: you love Jesus.
ANDREW (*To Ahn*): Ma? Ma?
ELIZABETH: Andrew, wake up.
ANDREW: Sorry, I thought I heard . . .
ELIZABETH: Did you just say, "Ma?"
AHN: Andrew—what this I hear, you no want baby?
ANDREW: It's okay, go back to sleep.

(Elizabeth goes back to sleep. Ahn sits on the edge of the bed.)

AHN: Andrew.

ANDREW: Shit! You're a Christian, Ma. Christians don't come back from the dead.

AHN: You forget—I am *Chinese* Christian. Best of East, best of West.

ANDREW: Yeah, worst of both worlds, don't remind me. What are you doing here, anyway?

AHN: To become grandmother—why I must wait so long? Now I must help you . . . so you not make terrible mistake.

ANDREW: Ma, I've never wanted to become a father. This pregnancy—it happened by accident.

AHN: This may be last chance God give you—to make new life.

ANDREW: You were always hounding me: have children, go to church, follow Jesus' plan. I've never wanted anything to do with that sort of life.

AHN: You never go church, this your third wife. Already you prove you are big sinner. Now, baby—on the way, Andrew. Time to cast out demon of your anger. Time you hear my story again—not with ear only, but also with spirit.

ANDREW: Sorry, but that's the last thing I need right now.

AHN: No—is only thing you need.

ANDREW: To hear how you became a religious fanatic? No thanks, I think it's time for you to get back to heaven. *(Shakes Elizabeth)* Elizabeth—

(Elizabeth sits up in bed. She's wearing ghost makeup and robes, and speaks in the voice of Eling, Third Wife, a Chinese woman in her early twenties.)

ELING: The spirit of my unborn child cries out to be remembered.

(Eling exits. Luan, a woman in her thirties, appears.)

LUAN: Ah Ying! Tell the servants to begin the feast for Husband's arrival!

(Siu-Yong, a woman in her forties, appears.)

SIU-YONG: Third Wife—you are responsible for seeing to it that the village is scrubbed and whitewashed.

(Ahn produces a Chinese man's robe from the early twentieth century. She slips it onto Andrew, and he becomes Eng Tieng-Bin, his grandfather.)

AHN: Remember? When you are little boy? You lie on my stomach, and I tell you story of our family. Winter of 1918. My father, Tieng-Bin, he make this family chosen by God. *(Pause)* My father work in Philippine, make money. But like all oversea Chinese, he leave behind most important part of life—his three wife, his children— *(Ahn begins to speak in the voice of a ten-year-old girl)* —all your future, Papa, you left behind in China. So after three years away, you got on a steamer ship, barreling across the South China Sea, towards our home village near the port of Amoy, in the province of Fukien.

SIU-YONG: Ahn! Ahn—where are you?

(Ahn exits with Andrew/Tieng-Bin. Lights come up, revealing the home of Eng Tieng-Bin. The living room of the Main Hall, surrounded in a semi-circle by three pavilions. Luan stands over a Servant.)

LUAN *(To Servant)***:** What are you doing? Perhaps you don't wish to work in this house any longer? You would rather starve to death like your brothers and sisters, is that it?

(Eling enters.)

ELING: No, Second Wife! He was only following my orders.

LUAN: You act as if I was going to beat him personally. You forget, Third Wife—some of us in this house were raised as ladies.

ELING: Maybe you should talk to First Wife about this.

LUAN: Who can wait for her? There're a hundred tasks I have to complete before Husband's return. And this waste of his mother's milk failed to carry out my orders!

ELING: First Wife said I could use him to whitewash the village.

LUAN: She didn't tell me. And what is First Wife doing—reassigning domestics? That sort of disorder only confuses their simple minds.

(Siu-Yong enters.)

SIU-YONG: Second Wife, no one creates disorder like you.

LUAN AND ELING: First Wife!

SIU-YONG: You can hear the bickering all the way across the compound. I don't care if you cut each other to ribbons, at least have the good taste to keep your voices down. What is the problem now?

ELING: She was about to punish—!

LUAN: He disobeyed my orders!

ELING: You said he could help me!

LUAN: I need all the staff I can get!

SIU-YONG: You two could give the goddess of mercy herself a headache.

(Ahn enters, as a ten-year-old girl.)

(To Ahn) Ahn, go play with your brothers and sisters. Your aunties are making peace—which is never a pretty sight.

AHN: Second Auntie, are you causing trouble again?

SIU-YONG: You must respect your auntie as a true source of wisdom. I don't care how irritating she is. Now apologize to her, or I'll have you whipped. *(Pause)* Did you hear me?

LUAN: She knows you won't whip her. You never whip her. No one whips anyone around here anymore.

(Luan crosses to Ahn, slaps her.)

SIU-YONG: Now what are you doing?

LUAN: Just helping you honor tradition, First Wife.

SIU-YONG: You have no right to strike my child! Only her nanny can do that!
   (To Ahn) Ahn, go. And stop whimpering—you shouldn't give her the satisfaction. *(To Servant)* Ah Ti! Go!

(Ahn and Servant exit.)

Listen—our Husband has been away three years, and he will return to find his wives filled with love and cooperation—no matter how we feel about one another, is that clear?

LUAN: I guess I'm just too honest for that. Hypocrisy sickens me.

SIU-YONG: If you can't live with dishonesty, you have no business calling yourself a woman. Now—settle your dispute as true sisters. Or I may decide to find our Husband a Fourth Wife.

ELING: Dearest Elder Sister, forgive me for my disrespect. I know I will never be able to match the great wisdom you have gained from having lived so many more years on this earth than me.

LUAN: Thank you, Little Sister. Forgive *me*. When husband made you his concubine, I took a solemn vow never to remind you of your peasant birth, or the fact that you were originally brought here to be my servant. I only pray that one day you will manage to bear him a child.

SIU-YONG: That's what I like around here. True harmony. Now, everyone—back to work!

(*The women exit separately. The pavilions are illuminated, revealing the three wives burning offerings to their parents. Ahn attends Siu-Yong in her pavilion.*)

(*To her altar*) Papa, Mama—on days like today, I feel like running away from all my obligations. Thank heaven for duty. Without it, we would be forced to think for ourselves.

(*She burns ghost money**) First, here's some money for you to wave in the faces of the other ghosts. Thank the heavens for inventing money—without it, what would we use to measure love? (*She holds up paper dolls*) And here are more servants—in case you were forced to beat the last bunch to death.

(*She pulls out an unrecognizable paper item*) And— what have we here? Ahn made these herself.

AHN: It's a steamer ship. Like the one Papa's riding on.

SIU-YONG: Oh, Ahn.

AHN: They want it. They want to be modern—like Papa.

SIU-YONG: You think you know your father so well?

AHN: From his letters. He likes modern things—not like you.

SIU-YONG: The fact that something is new simply means it has not had time to disappoint us.

AHN: Papa says, in the modern world—that they don't make girls wear bindings on their feet.

SIU-YONG: Do you want to end up a lonely spinster? Now, listen. Your father spends his time abroad trading with monkeys and devils; he may come home with all sorts of new ideas. Don't be too easily impressed.

(*She burns a paper steamer ship*) Papa, Mama, hear

---

*Ghost money is imitation money specifically intended for offerings to the dead.

my prayer—let Husband return, if it is possible, a normal man.

LUAN *(To her altar)*: Papa, I forgive you for losing all our money, and even for selling me to be a Second Wife. All I ask in return is that Husband see myself and my son as we are: selfless, humble and modest. And reward us with absolute power.

ELING *(To her altar; burning paper robes)*: Papa, Mama—here are the silk robes you never wore in life. With Husband away, life has been hard. But what's made it bearable is the chance to give you nice things. And, please, let Husband look at me with the same eyes as when he left.

(The lights fade on the ladies' pavilions, and come up on Tieng-Bin, who enters, and kneels before the altar of his ancestors.)

TIENG-BIN: Papa, Mama, Ankong, Ama—I know I haven't been the most diligent son lately. *(He kowtows, burns paper money)* But how can I explain—what it is like for me to work in the modern world—and then return here, to my home village, where everything remains as you and your fathers decided it should be? Can you possibly understand—you who lived your entire lives within the boundaries of this country hamlet, so far removed from any threat to your old ways? *(Pause)* Then what do I do with my doubts? Questions concerning the very traditions you taught me? When I was young, Papa, you would order me to obey, and your strong hand put an end to all discussion. How much simpler life was in those days.

(He pulls out a small crucifix, displays it to the altar) I bought a souvenir for you from a Christian temple in the Philippines. A naked man nailed to some boards. They told me for good luck, you can kiss its feet. They're very strange, the Westerners, and yet—hopeful, too. All the time talking about new inventions, new ideas. Nothing seems to excite them more than the future.

(Chinese folk music plays.)

Well, I must prepare for the banquet. Don't worry, I am still a good son. I go through all the motions, and curse myself for every deviation. In the house of his birth, a man is always a child.

(In the dimly lit Main Hall, Tieng-Bin and the ladies enact a stylized greeting ritual. They sit and begin to eat. Ahn rushes in from offstage, jumps into Tieng-Bin's lap. Lights up, music out.)

Hey, hey—who is this?

AHN: Who do you think? It's Ahn, remember? And you are my papa.

SIU-YONG: Ahn—get back to your table.

TIENG-BIN: No, you couldn't be Ahn. You must be some impostor!

AHN: But I *am* Ahn. What's wrong with you?

SIU-YONG *(To Ahn):* Now!

TIENG-BIN: Ahn is just a baby. This person in my lap is a young lady.

AHN: Well . . . if you won't believe me, then you're just ignorant.

TIENG-BIN: Oh, that mouth! You *must* be Ahn!

AHN: That's what I've been trying to—

LUAN: Dear Husband, would you like to see the rest of the children, now?

SIU-YONG *(To Luan):* No! We don't want her setting a bad example for the other children.

LUAN: It's a little late for that, don't you think?

TIENG-BIN *(To Ahn):* See the trouble you cause? Why can't you present yourself with your brothers and sisters?

AHN: Because I am a Golden Child. Kang told me so.

TIENG-BIN: Kang?

SIU-YONG *(To Tieng-Bin):* Her nanny's husband.

AHN: He took me gambling. Kang says he always loses, but with me beside him, he beat the whole table. So he told me I am a Golden Child.

TIENG-BIN: I need all the luck I can get. Perhaps I should take you back to the Philippines, huh?

AHN: Would that mean I could take the bindings off my feet?

SIU-YONG: Ahn!

AHN: My feet hurt so bad at night—and they stink, too!

SIU-YONG: No one ever said that feminine beauty was pretty.

AHN: It's okay. I wouldn't mind. I *want* to end up a lonely spinster.

TIENG-BIN: None of my daughters are going to end up spinsters, understand? *(To Ahn)* The world is changing. There's a whole new generation of men who will want an educated wife. Not some backwards girl hobbling around on rotting feet, filling the room with the stench of death!

(Silence; wives stare at Tieng-Bin.)

Ahn, go now.

(Ahn exits.)

First Wife—next time, I should greet the children before the banquet begins.

SIU-YONG: Of course. I hope our humble dinner meets with your satisfaction.

TIENG-BIN: Oh, yes. Yes! The . . . roast pig, it gets better every time. When I'm in the Philippines, all I can think of is the way you make sticky rice in this village.

SIU-YONG: All credit must be given to Second Wife. The feast was her arrangement exclusively.

TIENG-BIN: Second Wife, you honor me with your gracious attention.

LUAN: Please, Husband. This is a task any child could've performed as well as I. But your son, Yung-Bin—he is such a brilliant young scholar, his tutor tells me he can barely keep up with him . . .

SIU-YONG: Yes, we often see him chasing Yung-Bin across the courtyard.

LUAN: I cannot accept the suggestion that I possess even a shred of ability. The air itself is wasted on the likes of me.

(Tieng-Bin leads a toast to the smiling Luan.)

TIENG-BIN: To Second Wife—

LUAN: Oh, stop!—

TIENG-BIN: —full of diligent support for your loving sisters.

LUAN: Stop talking about me . . . This is more than I can take—to a woman of my upbringing, all this praise is sheer torture—

(Siu-Yong turns to Eling.)

SIU-YONG: And did you see, dear Husband—?

ELING: First Wife! Don't!

SIU-YONG: —the brilliance of our village?

TIENG-BIN: Why, of course. The streets, they nearly shine—

ELING: No, no—there're spots and stains all over—

TIENG-BIN: When I stepped off the boat, I said: "What? Is this the Forbidden City? Or America, where the streets are paved with gold?"

ELING: You're so kind to ignore my horrible—

SIU-YONG *(To Eling):* Shut your mouth!

    (To Tieng-Bin) Some afternoons, I look out from my pavilion, and there she is, scrubbing the dung off the road as if she were still a peasant!

ELING: Once! Once, I saw some.

TIENG-BIN: To Third Wife—

ELING: So, I scooped it up, that's all.

TIENG-BIN: On every surface of this village, I see your goodness reflected.

(Tieng-Bin raises his cup. Eling points to Siu-Yong before they can drink.)

ELING: No—First Wife!
TIENG-BIN: Please—
ELING: She deserves all the credit.
SIU-YONG: Third Wife! Take your praise bravely, no matter how painful it might be!

(They drink, then Tieng-Bin adds:)

TIENG-BIN: To Eling—the sweetest and most fragrant flower.

(They drink again.)

ELING: No, no, no, no—could you all please talk about someone else, now?
LUAN: Husband, Third Wife is correct to shine the light on First Wife. Without her leadership—
SIU-YONG: Hey, hey! Stop that!
LUAN: —this entire village would've rotted away, and the first rain washed it out to sea.
SIU-YONG: What are you—retarded?
LUAN: First Wife—you said we must bear our praise bravely—
SIU-YONG: But you deserve yours.
LUAN: First Wife inspires us to work together, in the spirit of true sisterly affection.
SIU-YONG: Your mother should've drowned you before you learned to speak.
LUAN: To put aside petty feelings and focus on our common goal. Truly, First Wife supplies the wisdom which holds together this sisterhood, this family and this entire village.
SIU-YONG: Bitch.

(Tieng-Bin raises his glass toward Siu-Yong.)

TIENG-BIN: I'm well aware of what you're saying about your
older sister. In my absence, she is forced to be both
Wife and Husband. To First Wife—who blesses this
home with wisdom.

(They drink to Siu-Yong.)

SIU-YONG: Why don't you pick up a knife and plunge it into
my heart?

(They sit and resume eating.)

Nothing like a round of compliments to work up an
appetite.

TIENG-BIN: I guess this is as good a time as any to share with
you some of what I've been thinking lately.

SIU-YONG: Husband, we rely on you to bring home thoughts
from the darkest corners of the world.

TIENG-BIN: On the boat, I met a man—an Englishman, a
Christian missionary. We began talking—mostly out of
curiosity. After all, the founder of our Chinese
Republic, Dr. Sun Yat-Sen—he studied both Western
medicine and Christianity. At any rate, this man—
Reverend Baines—has come to run a mission here in
Amoy. I've invited him over to continue our discussion.
(Pause) Don't worry—I don't intend to become a
Christian. But it's important to learn about new ideas—
following the example of Dr. Sun.

SIU-YONG: Perhaps, then, you will also study medicine as
well?

TIENG-BIN: Well, I—maybe if I were younger, I . . . that's a
good one.

SIU-YONG: Funny the difference between Chinese and
Occidental people. In China, we leave food at the altar
for others. The white devils, they go to the altar and fill
themselves with free bread and wine.

(The women laugh.)

TIENG-BIN: No, that's not—that's a stereotype! I wish you wouldn't act so ignorant.

SIU-YONG: Forgive us, Honored Husband. We are just backward women—hobbling around on rotting feet.

(Pause.)

TIENG-BIN: Look . . . what I said to Ahn—about the feet— I certainly wasn't thinking about any of you.

SIU-YONG: Oh no, of course not. The idea never even occurred to us.

LUAN: I don't even remember what you said to Ahn.

SIU-YONG: Husband is too sensitive on our behalf.

LUAN: I, for one, am very interested to hear what this reverend has to say. Perhaps I can join you sometime.

TIENG-BIN: That's not necessary, Second Wife, I don't expect you to—

LUAN: But I agree with you. I don't like the old ways.

TIENG-BIN: If the reverend comes, you're all welcome to join us. But don't feel any pressure.

LUAN: C'mon, Sisters! What've we got to lose?

SIU-YONG: Second Wife, I am constantly amazed by your rigid flexibility.

(Tieng-Bin claps his hands.)

TIENG-BIN: Now—a bit of the modern world for you each to call your own.

(Servants enter, bearing three gifts covered with cloth.)

Ah Ying! *(Servant lifts cloth off Siu-Yong's gift, revealing a cuckoo clock)*

SIU-YONG: Oh, my—what a clever Occidental clock!

TIENG-BIN: Here, let me . . . *(He moves forward the minute hand, causing the cuckoo to appear)* The mechanical bird comes out every hour. I thought it would be charming, hanging on your wall.

SIU-YONG: Yes, I'm sure it will do wonders for my insomnia.

TIENG-BIN: Ah Tsun! (*He signals another servant, who carries a gift to Luan*)

LUAN: Husband, you didn't forget me?

TIENG-BIN: An ocean away, Second Wife, I found you impossible to forget.

(*Servant removes cloth, revealing Luan's gift: a waffle iron.*)

LUAN: Oh! It's so . . . shiny. What is it?

TIENG-BIN: It's a waffle iron—it makes pastries that white men eat for breakfast. I assumed—since you prepare the banquets, that you would appreciate—

LUAN: I do! In fact, it's so beautiful, I can hardly imagine actually using it.

TIENG-BIN: Good! And now—Ah Ti! (*Servant reveals Eling's gift: a phonograph player*) This is perhaps the best the outside world has to offer. (*He slips on a 78—a scratchy recording of* La Traviata) Western opera. A bit difficult to appreciate at first.

LUAN: It's so . . . primitive, so crude and barbaric. I like it!

TIENG-BIN: This is called *La Traviata*. The story of two lovers who only wish to be together—but their society makes this impossible.

SIU-YONG: I can see why.

TIENG-BIN: Now—I've spent three years away from the children; I won't wait a second longer. Go!

(*Ladies start to exit.*)

LUAN (*Calling off*): Ah Ying! Warn Yung-Bin we're coming!

(*Luan and Siu-Yong exit. Tieng-Bin grabs Eling before she can exit. He gives her a long kiss.*)

ELING: Thank you.

TIENG-BIN: For what?

ELING: For answering my prayers.

(She exits after the other women. Lights cross-fade onto Luan's pavilion. She is performing her toilette. Siu-Yong enters.)

LUAN: First Wife, aren't you supposed to be announced?

SIU-YONG: For years, you've made fun of my policy against whipping. Well, strip off your robe and come to the courtyard.

LUAN: You're growing soft.

SIU-YONG: What are you talking about?

LUAN: Even your threats don't have the usual conviction behind them.

SIU-YONG: Tonight, at dinner—you went too far.

LUAN: Really?

SIU-YONG: I won't allow it.

LUAN: Husband didn't seem to mind.

SIU-YONG: It is the simplest thing to manipulate a man. Just call him your master, and he's your slave for life.

LUAN: I, for one, trust my Husband's judgment.

SIU-YONG: How could you? Inviting us to listen to the black magic of some European witch doctor—putting us on the spot like that—

LUAN: I had to do something. *You* certainly weren't controlling the situation.

SIU-YONG: Me?

LUAN: You let Third Wife run wild! Far beyond her proper place at the table.

SIU-YONG: She hardly spoke a word all evening.

LUAN: Of course, I understand—the two of you have struck a bargain against me.

SIU-YONG: If there's one thing I try to be, it's fair-minded.

LUAN: And so you dishonored me at the table before our Husband—

SIU-YONG: I went to great lengths to praise you!

LUAN: —allowing Third Wife to go on forever, until he had to offer her two toasts instead of one!

SIU-YONG: So?

LUAN: One toast should've been more than enough for a slave, a concubine—but no, she went on, protesting, blushing, denying—that slut. Her modesty was absolutely shameless. And you just sat there!

SIU-YONG: I don't know why you keep track of such—

LUAN: Don't act stupid, Sister. You, of all people, should know—humility is power.

SIU-YONG: You could've gotten toasted twice. Why didn't *you* keep protesting your unworthiness? Should I punish Third Wife because she showed a little initiative?

LUAN: I don't flaunt my submissiveness like some people.

SIU-YONG: You know what your problem is? Deep inside, you believe the flattery is true.

LUAN: And Third Wife is different?

SIU-YONG: She's not smart enough to conceal her real emotions.

LUAN: Then why is she the one sharing her bed with Husband on his first night home?

SIU-YONG: You can't possibly take that sort of thing personally!

LUAN: I won't be content with her soggy leftovers.

SIU-YONG: Husbands always go to the bed of the youngest wife. That's what they're for. To save the rest of us all that mess and fuss.

LUAN: Has it ever occurred to you, that our Husband is different?

SIU-YONG: And that's your excuse for putting us in this position?

LUAN: If Husband becomes a Christian, then everything changes. All roles around here are up for reassignment. And the one who breaks the most rules wins.

SIU-YONG: Foreigners have been invading our country for centuries. We always change them more than they change us. It won't be any different this time.

LUAN: I'm trying to warn you, Older Sister, because I despise Third Wife even more than you. You—I find myself starting to pity.

SIU-YONG: What will it take to have some real peace in this house?

(From offstage, the recording of La Traviata *is heard.)*

LUAN: Listen. They're playing that Italian opera. He brings her music, and me a gift for the cooks.

SIU-YONG: So? I've got a bird that tells the time whether I wish to know or not.

LUAN: If it's modern Husband wants, he's looking in the wrong pavilion. No one in this house will be more modern than me ever again.

(Pause. They listen to the music from the adjoining pavilion.)

SIU-YONG: When you first came to this house, I watched Husband go to your bed and never complained. Why can't you do the same?

LUAN: When he started coming to my room, you took up the pipe.

SIU-YONG: So? I thought I'd finally earned the right to some real pleasure.

LUAN: I refuse to start taking drugs.

SIU-YONG: If you're determined to destroy yourself, there's nothing I can do to help you.

LUAN: That's why you can't see what's going on under your nose.

SIU-YONG: Stay away from the preacher. If you try to show me up by becoming a Christian, I'll see to it that you're demoted to a common concubine.

LUAN: I'm not certain I can make any such promises, First Wife.

SIU-YONG: You don't understand—the pipe makes me stronger, not weaker. It takes away the only thing that stands in the way of a woman's power—our feelings.

(*Siu-Yong exits. Luan, hearing the music, looks toward Eling's pavilion.*)

LUAN: No, *you* don't understand. Right now, feeling is the only thing our Husband desires.

(*Lights fade on Luan, and come up on Eling and Tieng-Bin.*)

ELING: You shouldn't have praised me so much in front of the other wives. Second Wife will be fuming for weeks.
TIENG-BIN: But—just looking at you across the dinner table . . .
ELING: Are you going to make me blush again?
TIENG-BIN: I would never have believed my eyes could give me so much pleasure.
ELING: Just your eyes? What about your other senses?
TIENG-BIN: Well, you see, I thought I'd try out this new form of Western self-restraint.
ELING: What kind of ridiculous—? (*She reaches for him. He pulls away*)
TIENG-BIN: I'm restricting my intake of physical pleasures.
ELING: By now, your pleasure should be just about ready to explode.
TIENG-BIN: I've been living among the Christians, remember?
ELING: What does that have to do—?
TIENG-BIN: They consider abstinence a great virtue.
ELING: Says who? I hear white men stuff money into their pockets and meat down their thick throats.
TIENG-BIN: Don't be so close-minded—
ELING: Oh? Am I not—what?—*modern* enough for you? You already insulted my feet tonight.
TIENG-BIN: I'm sorry. That was just a slip of the tongue.

ELING: Where I come from, insults always get punished.

(Keeping her back to him, she crosses to the phonograph, sashaying seductively as she walks.)

So—you only want to watch? Like a good Christian? You say you are a modern man who wants a modern wife?

(Eling removes her robe, revealing Western lingerie.)

TIENG-BIN: Where did you get that outfit?

ELING: From the catalog. I've been so busy improving myself. *(Pause)* I like being modern, too. I like my new phonograph player. *(Begins to dance to the music, keeping her back to him)* I like this *Traviata*. It fills me with feelings. Modern feelings. Delicious feelings of . . . power.

(Tieng-Bin rises to his feet, starts toward her.)

No, no, no. Self-denial. Like a good Christian . . .

TIENG-BIN: Eling . . .

ELING: I'm your slave, remember? I can only obey your wishes. *(Eling eludes him)*

TIENG-BIN: What are you—? You're going to kill me! . . .

ELING: You must be able to hold out longer than that, Honored Husband.

TIENG-BIN: I haven't touched a woman in three years!

ELING: You expect me to believe that? The prostitutes in Manila must be for shit.

TIENG-BIN: That's enough!

ELING: My lord and master . . . Sit!

TIENG-BIN: Eling!

ELING: Now, be modern. Sit! You wait for me to come to you. *(Pause)* When you're away, I would put this on and imagine your face as you lowered the straps from my shoulders . . .

TIENG-BIN: Now, you don't have to imagine any longer . . .

ELING: Not yet. Will you please struggle for me a little longer?

TIENG-BIN: But . . . why?

ELING: I don't know. It lets me know you care. That you suffer for me . . . like I suffer for you.

TIENG-BIN: Don't you believe that I want to spend every night here with you?

ELING: Yes, but you have your duty to the other wives.

TIENG-BIN: Eling . . . you are the first woman I was ever able to choose for myself . . . and you will be the last.

ELING: Now, if you like, you may touch me.

(He kisses her.)

You know I'm going to pay for every one of these kisses.

TIENG-BIN: What are you—?

ELING: When you're away, Second Wife bursts into my room whenever she feels like it, breaks—

TIENG-BIN: Eling, please. At least here, let's not talk about the others. I want to think only of you—as if you were my only wife.

ELING: That sounds so naughty.

TIENG-BIN: You're the one person from whom I want to have no secrets. This is my fantasy: that we will speak only words which are true.

ELING: Then can I tell you my secret? *(Pause)* I like it. That you come to me—that you look at me different from the other wives . . . I like it.

TIENG-BIN: Then look back at me. Don't avert your gaze, but look me straight in the eye. Watch me, watching you.

(They look into each other's eyes. Tieng-Bin and Eling fall into the bed, as lights fade. Lights come up on Siu-Yong's pavilion. She blows smoke from her opium pipe at her family altar.)

SIU-YONG (*Smoking on pipe; to altar*)**:** Papa . . . here's something special for you tonight. Mama, you too. A new blend made from Indian and Burmese poppies. It turns the worst insults of other wives into beautiful poetry. (*Pause*) I know I've neglected you in the days since Husband's return. But can you blame me? I prayed for normal, and what walks into my home? A bloody pagan.

(*Ahn appears in the doorway to Siu-Yong's pavilion.*)

Here you are . . . come, come. (*Ahn crosses slowly. Siu-Yong puts her pipe down. She pulls Ahn down toward her*) Daughter—you've stopped visiting me these past few nights.

AHN: I've been getting up early. To spend time with Papa.

SIU-YONG: You are a good daughter. Headstrong, but I'll tell you a secret—I like that. Later in years, when you grow breasts and hips, you will learn to appear obedient. But you will always remember a time when your tongue was unbound. (*Pause*) I think it's wonderful that you spend time with Papa. In fact, that's why I called you here tonight. I think you should see him even more often.

AHN: Really?

SIU-YONG: Your Papa has invited a guest to visit, a white demon with skin the color of a day-old corpse. This man makes his living speaking nonsense.

AHN: Like a clown?

SIU-YONG: Only he doesn't know it. He is a clown who thinks he is a god. (*Pause*) When this clown comes, Second Auntie will join them, to try and win your father to her side. I want you there, also—to tell me everything she does.

AHN: When Papa's talking grown-up things, he always sends me away.

SIU-YONG: Just pretend you, too, wish to learn some of this rubbish. Your father will be so impressed that his daughter wishes to become a "modern woman." *(Ahn backs away from the altar)* Where are you going?

AHN: I . . . I don't want to lie to Papa.

SIU-YONG: You refuse your own mother? And the ghosts of all your ancestors? They're already very angry with you.

AHN: Why?

SIU-YONG: Because you complained about your foot-bindings at the banquet.

AHN: Do you think they like it when you smoke? I think you should stop.

SIU-YONG: I smoke for strength to carry out their wishes. But you—you would rather Second Auntie take over this house.

AHN: That's not true!

SIU-YONG: All right. Then you are the one who must stop her.

AHN: Why me?

SIU-YONG: Because you are a Golden Child. You said so yourself, remember? Well, if you're any sort of Golden Child at all, you should be able to hear the voices of the dead.

AHN: I don't know if I—maybe I don't want to hear them.

SIU-YONG: Ahn! To preserve the family is your first duty as a woman. If you fail, your children and grandchildren will abandon you in your old age; and when you die, your face will fade slowly from their memories, and your name will be forgotten.

AHN: Wait. I . . . I think I can hear them . . .

SIU-YONG: Of course you can.

AHN: They're saying . . . they're saying, "Don't be afraid . . ."

SIU-YONG: That sounds about right.

AHN: They're saying, "We will help you . . . make you brave . . . so you can save your whole family."

SIU-YONG: Good. You see, you are a special child. You're my daughter.

(Lights fade on scene. Lights come up on Tieng-Bin's altar. He burns offerings.)

TIENG-BIN *(To altar)*: Papa, Mama—the servants found some flowers today, which had somehow blossomed in winter. I thought you might appreciate them.

(Luan enters.)

LUAN: Husband!

TIENG-BIN: Second Wife!

LUAN: Excuse me—I didn't know you were here.

TIENG-BIN: It's hard to believe anything in this house escapes your notice.

LUAN: Oh, you flatter me. Do you mind? *(She sits beside him)*

TIENG-BIN: Actually, I was just—

LUAN: I usually come at dawn to tend your parents' altar. But last night, I couldn't sleep. Did you hear poor Ahn, crying in her room?

TIENG-BIN: Yes, I did.

LUAN: I understand First Wife recently tightened her foot-bindings.

TIENG-BIN: I thought as much.

LUAN: Husband, I am so grateful that you spoke out against foot-binding at the banquet the other night. But I must tell you, afterward, First Wife came to my pavilion hysterical, railing against everything you said.

TIENG-BIN: I don't expect First Wife to agree with me.

LUAN: As for myself, the idea of having a daughter—with beautiful, gigantic feet—it excites me. Do you want that . . . as much as I do?

TIENG-BIN: Actually, I do. To come home once more and see children—being turned into cripples—it makes me ashamed to be Chinese.

LUAN: I *knew* you would agree!

TIENG-BIN: Now, excuse me.

(Luan rises to leave; then:)

LUAN: Husband. Perhaps you would honor me later tonight?

(Luan exits.)

TIENG-BIN *(To altar)***:** Papa, Mama—do I go to her? As obligation demands? Look at her—most men would jump at the opportunity. It's just that making love to Luan feels so much like doing business. And yet when it comes to foot-binding, Second Wife seems more willing to change than I. *(He calls to a servant)* At Tsun! *(To altar)* Why should we cling to a tradition that only passes down suffering from one generation to the next?

(Servant enters. To Servant:)

Fetch First Wife.

(Servant exits. To altar:)

Every day I let pass without acting, only makes the damage worse. Oh, I can hear you—and all the ancestors—crying from beyond, "Some things cannot be changed." But don't I have the right to try? I accept all responsibility, assume all consequences.

(Siu-Yong enters.)

SIU-YONG: Husband?
TIENG-BIN: It's an outdated, barbaric custom, and I won't allow it any longer.
SIU-YONG: What custom, Honored—?

(Ahn enters separately, eavesdrops from a concealed location.)

TIENG-BIN: From this day onward, foot-binding is forbidden in this home and the village beyond. I want you to remove Ahn's bindings.
SIU-YONG: One thing I have never doubted, Husband: that you are a good man.

TIENG-BIN: Let's not begin with the flattery.

SIU-YONG: Remove her bindings, and you will rescue her from pain. Isn't that your thinking?

TIENG-BIN: Do you have a point to make?

SIU-YONG: Some pains are necessary in the life of a woman. In order to spare her a lifetime of loneliness.

TIENG-BIN: All that is changing! The new government has already outlawed the practice.

SIU-YONG: Tell me, Husband—would *you* marry a woman with unbound feet? *(Pause)* For the sake of your daughter, answer truthfully. *(Pause)* Men. You dream of changing the world when you cannot even change yourselves. *(Pause)* Now—may I go while you consider the matter further?

(Siu-Yong starts to exit. Ahn reveals herself.)

AHN: Papa—I don't want to wear them.

(Pause.)

TIENG-BIN: Remove her bindings. Now!

SIU-YONG: Once the foot is half-trained, to release it back to its natural state—her agony will be multiplied twofold.

TIENG-BIN: If you won't obey, I will do it myself!

SIU-YONG: At least allow us to be alone.

(Mother and daughter step into Siu-Yong's pavilion. Tieng-Bin remains in the courtyard. Overlapping ghost voices fade up. Tieng-Bin hears the spirits of his ancestors.)

GHOST VOICES:

To betray your ancestors is to cut your own heart from your body.

The undutiful son reaps a harvest of famine and ruin.

Those who forsake the past enter the future without a tongue to speak or eyes to see.

His children and his children's children will be cursed
to the seventh generation.
Only a fool turns his back on the wisdom of the ages.
All things worth saying have already been spoken. All
things worth knowing have already been made known.

SIU-YONG *(To Ahn)*: Daughter—you do not know what a terrible gift is freedom.

(Siu-Yong unwinds strips of cloth from Ahn's feet. In the courtyard, Tieng-Bin listens to Ahn's cries of pain.)

TIENG-BIN *(To altar)*: Papa, Mama—forgive me.

(Lights fade on scene. Lights up on courtyard. Chinese folk instrumental music underscores a pantomime scene: Luan, Eling and Siu-Yong enter the courtyard to play mah-jongg. A servant brings in a calling card. Siu-Yong looks at it, the women scatter to their respective pavilions. Reverend Baines, a white man in his fifties, enters. Separately, Andrew enters with Ahn, who is again his mother, an old woman.)

AHN: Andrew—when reverend come, this first time ever I
see my mother hide from any person. My father fight—
bring change to our home. But when change come,
come like fire. No one know—who will live, and who
will be lost. *(Pause)* This, first foreigner, ever I see.
White demon!

(Fade to black.)

ACT TWO

Light comes up on Ahn as a young girl, running and jumping toward the Main Hall. Then area lights come up on the Main Hall, revealing Tieng-Bin and Reverend Baines sitting over tea and pastries. Ahn enters and sits on the floor. Baines speaks brokenly with an English accent.

TIENG-BIN: Oolong.

BAINES: Oolong.

TIENG-BIN: Jasmine.

BAINES: Jasmine.

TIENG-BIN: Monkey-pick.

BAINES: Monkey-pick?

TIENG-BIN: Oolong and jasmine form the bulk of our export. But monkey-pick tea is the pride of the province.

BAINES: Why you call—?

TIENG-BIN: Because it's picked by monkeys, why else?

BAINES: I . . . no understand.

TIENG-BIN: The leaf grows so high that only monkeys can reach it. So we train them to harvest the plant for us.

Something like among your people, I understand, there
is a fungus that only pigs can dig up.

BAINES: Oh. Yes. Uh, uh—no can say in Chinese. But, not
my people.

TIENG-BIN: No?

BAINES: No. I—English. Pigs—French.

TIENG-BIN: Oh, yes, yes. You're separated by a large chan-
nel of water.

BAINES: No large enough.

TIENG-BIN: We feel the same way about the Japanese.
(*He toasts*) To understanding.

BAINES: Understanding. Yes, yes.

(*They drink.*)

Oh, oh—very good. Mmmm. Yummy. England, we cannot drink such very good tea.

TIENG-BIN: Well, you lack properly trained monkeys.

BAINES: Mon—? Oh, oh. Yes! I even learn—not to add the
cream.

TIENG-BIN: Please! You might as well add cream to wine!

BAINES: Ha, ha! Tea such yummy, no need cream . . . and . . . ?
(*He points to the plate on the table*)

TIENG-BIN: Dan tat.

BAINES: Dan tat.

TIENG-BIN: I had a special batch made up, in honor of your
visit.

BAINES: Ahn, please—you come . . . also cake eat?

(*Ahn crosses to Baines, takes a pastry.*)

TIENG-BIN: Ahn! What do you say to the reverend?

BAINES: Please—not my house.

TIENG-BIN: You've been coming to visit us for many months.

BAINES: Not my cake.

TIENG-BIN: She must show you proper respect.

AHN (*To Baines*): Thank you. "Yummy?" (*She pops it into her
mouth*)

BAINES: Yes. Yummy. Very yummy.

(*He does the same. She resumes her position on the floor.*)

TIENG-BIN: I have to be honest with you, Reverend—
BAINES: Mmmm.
TIENG-BIN: I deal with a lot of white men in my business. Americans, Englishmen, Scots, Australians—
BAINES: No, no . . . Australians—we no think they white men.
TIENG-BIN: Well, we don't claim them as Asians, either.
BAINES: Again—understanding.

(*They drink.*)

TIENG-BIN: Most of the white men I meet—we do business, but deep inside, I know they look down on me.
BAINES: Mmmm.
TIENG-BIN: And yet—when I listen to them talk, watch the way they deal with each other, I must admit—there's something about them I envy.
BAINES: Envy?
TIENG-BIN: Jealousy.
BAINES: Ah, yes.
TIENG-BIN: All of us are away from our families, Reverend. Do you understand what I am saying?
BAINES: Many . . . temptation?
TIENG-BIN: Let's be frank. Chinese or Christian—men away from their families—are still men. Understand?
BAINES: Temptation. Men. Yes, I understand.
TIENG-BIN: But . . . there's a difference between myself and the Westerners. They seem . . . more able to forget, to pretend, even to fall in love with these other women, far from home. Whereas I—I can never forget . . . that my life, my duty, lies here.
BAINES: You want forget? I think, Jesus no help you here.
TIENG-BIN: No, no, it's—how can I put this? It's not that I want to forget my family, quite the opposite. But to be Chinese—means to feel a whole web of obligation—

obligation?—dating back 5,000 years. I am afraid of dis-honoring my ancestors, even the ones dead for centuries. All the time, I feel ghosts—sitting on my back, whisper-ing in my ear—keeping me from living life as I see fit.

BAINES: I understand. Christian belief: we are all single per-son, is to say, all have own relation . . .

TIENG-BIN: Yes, I've seen this and it's remarkable. I'll tell you, Reverend—I once listened to some white sailors talking to each other. One said: "I can lift two hundred pounds." Another said: "I have an education." A third said: "In my life, I have saved a fortune." I was amazed.

BAINES: They brag. Not so nice.

TIENG-BIN: No, in a way, wonderful. That they feel so free to say who they are, without worrying that they're making someone else in the group feel small by their boasting.

BAINES: I see. In mission school, where learn me Chinese— they make—um, um—invent—new Chinese word, for new idea. Word is: individual.

TIENG-BIN: "Individual"?

BAINES: Meaning, each man, stand alone, choose own life.

TIENG-BIN: Yes, those sailors were individuals. Speaking the truth in their hearts, even if everyone around them dis-agreed!

BAINES: Okay. You try.

TIENG-BIN: What—what are you—?

BAINES: Like sailor. You try. You also, brag yourself.

TIENG-BIN: Reverend, c'mon. I mean, that sort of thing is interesting in theory, but—

BAINES: I start: my family, own many land—in beautiful country, name of Wales.

TIENG-BIN: Really? That's very impressive.

BAINES: No, no! I brag, you also. I go seminary, top of class! Now, you. You!

TIENG-BIN: I feel . . . okay, I run the largest Chinese-owned business in the Philippines. God, this is so—

BAINES: Good, good. God tell me: "Baines—you special man. Help China!"

TIENG-BIN: My peasants actually like me, because I try so hard to help them.

BAINES: Beautiful!

TIENG-BIN: This is incredibly self-indulgent.

BAINES: You like?

TIENG-BIN: Yes, I like.

BAINES: I am good good cook. Yummy!

TIENG-BIN: I employ good good cooks. Yummy! Yummy!

BAINES: I have daughter, most beautiful, all of world.

TIENG-BIN: One of my wives . . . is the most beautiful woman in the creation of any god. *(Pause)* What a luxury. To speak the truth—in my own home, of all places.

(Luan enters, dressed in Western clothing.)

LUAN: Just say the word, and I will disappear!

TIENG-BIN: Second Wife!

BAINES: Mrs. Eng—yummy!

LUAN: You are too kind, Reverend. You spoil a Chinese woman.

TIENG-BIN: You look so—

LUAN: Atrocious—

TIENG-BIN: —Exotic . . .

LUAN: I mean, who do I think I am?

TIENG-BIN: The mysterious Occidental.

BAINES: Very modern.

LUAN: I sent away for it about the time you started visiting us, Reverend.

BAINES: Me? Oh, oh . . . !

LUAN: You got us all very curious about Western ways.

TIENG-BIN: Did someone help you put that on?

LUAN: Yes, Cheng-Ming. Stupid girl. There're all sorts of strange support items—

BAINES: Oh?

LUAN: —for parts of the body that really should be able to support themselves.

BAINES: Please! Not for me hear, no, no!

LUAN: I'm sorry, was I being . . . immodest?

TIENG-BIN: From behind, you could be a typical white demon—oh, excuse me, Reverend.

BAINES: White demon—me—white demon.

LUAN: But I could never be as graceful as those Western women. To get into those shoes—did you realize, they actually walk on their toes?

BAINES: Chinese woman—no can?

LUAN *(To Baines)*: Well, you see, most of us lost our toes years ago . . .

BAINES: Oh . . . I see . . .

LUAN: Maybe I could give my Western shoes to Ahn, for when she's older.

TIENG-BIN: Second Wife! What a generous thought. *(To Ahn)* Ahn, what do you think of your auntie?

LUAN: I know what she'll say—I'm a freak.

BAINES: You look . . . like princess . . .

LUAN: What do *you* think, Husband?

TIENG-BIN: I'm amazed that you can transform yourself . . . into an entirely different person.

(Pause.)

LUAN: Reverend, has Husband taken care of your tea?

BAINES: Oh, yes, yes . . .

LUAN: And the dan tat?

BAINES: . . . so much, I eat like cow . . .

LUAN: You mean pig?

BAINES: Huh?

LUAN: Pig . . .

BAINES: Oh, yes, pig, pig—my Chinese . . .

LUAN: Your Chinese is excellent.

AHN: Auntie, may I have the shoes? Although I do not deserve them.

LUAN *(To Baines)*: Listen to her. It's so encouraging to see even Ahn influenced by your example. *(To Ahn)* Yes, you may have them. *(To Tieng-Bin)* Your son, Yung-Bin, has asked for a Western suit.

AHN: Can I see them—now?

LUAN (*To Baines*): So, Reverend, what lessons do you have for us today?

BAINES: Oh! Well . . .

AHN: I told the servants your story about the three wise men.

BAINES: My—my—? Ah, good!

TIENG-BIN: Amazing, isn't it? That her mind is so unfettered by the past.

LUAN: I am so fortunate Husband allows me to join you both. He is the most enlightened, most virtuous man in all of Fukien—no, in all of China.

TIENG-BIN: You praise me too much.

LUAN: Then let anyone in this house prove me wrong!

BAINES: He is great man—great man . . .

LUAN: This is what I like—honest talk! By thinking as he thinks—that's the Western way—the way of the future.

AHN: Second Auntie—

LUAN: The other wives, they don't feel so differently—

AHN: Second Auntie—

LUAN: Don't let the fact that they've never even said "hi" in eight months give you any other impression.

AHN: Second Auntie!

LUAN: What do you want!

AHN: I want my shoes!

TIENG-BIN: Ahn!

LUAN: Husband, will you please tell this girl selfishness is unworthy of your home? (*To Baines*) And it's not very Christian either, is it, Reverend?

BAINES: My Chinese . . . very bad . . .

LUAN: Well. I will forgo my lesson with the Reverend.

AHN (*To Luan*): You said I could have them.

TIENG-BIN: Luan, where are the shoes?

LUAN: They're in my pavilion. Please allow me to—

TIENG-BIN: No! I'll go. That way, you stay here, continue your lesson with the Reverend, and Ahn will get her shoes, too.

LUAN: I really don't mind—

TIENG-BIN: I'll settle this . . . as always. *(To Ahn)* Thank your auntie for her generous gift.

AHN: Thank you, Second Auntie.

TIENG-BIN: Excuse us, Reverend.

(Tieng-Bin exits.)

AHN: Precious Auntie, I'm sorry your feet are so dead and rotten.

(Ahn exits.)

LUAN: Do you have enough tea?

BAINES: Oh, yes . . . yes . . .

LUAN: Here, let me warm your cup—

BAINES: Thank you, so kind—

LUAN: You know, a traditional Chinese husband would never leave his wife alone with a strange man.

BAINES: I . . . strange?

LUAN: The strangest. You're a foreigner. For me to be sitting here, pouring tea for you, by Chinese standards—it is absolutely indecent.

BAINES: Ha, ha, ha . . . I no understand.

LUAN *(Offers a plate)*: Waffle? *(Baines declines)* He loves that daughter, favors her . . . of course, he has no choice, she's so demanding.

BAINES: Oh, Ahn! Yes, beautiful girl . . .

LUAN: Not by Chinese standards. It's her inner strength that impresses me. That she's managed to remain so brave with a mother who is an opium eater. *(Pause)* Bean cake?

BAINES: Opium? You say, opium? Drug? *(He mimes smoking a pipe)*

LUAN: Oh, no—I shouldn't have even opened my—

BAINES: Ahn's mama? Opium? Mr. Eng, does he—?

LUAN: My only interest is in helping First Wife recover . . . the drug makes her do things she doesn't mean—to plot against myself, my Husband . . . you . . .

BAINES: Me? First Wife plot against *me*?

LUAN: But if she were not a drug addict, I know—she would never force her daughter to spy against you!

BAINES: Please, slow. Ahn—is spy? How you know?

LUAN: The servants tell me everything.

BAINES: If this true. If Ahn is spy—

LUAN (*Starts to speak as if to a child*)**:** No—no get excited.

BAINES: Must tell Mr. Eng!

LUAN: No—please, instead, kill me!

BAINES: "Kill you"? What in devil are you—?

LUAN: Listen. If I tell Husband, he will not believe. Will become angry—at me, and you, also.

BAINES: So . . . no one tell him? But—

LUAN: No. Someone will tell him.

BAINES: Who?

LUAN: Third Wife—I told her Ahn is spy. She says, "I don't want to hear!" But—patience, one day, she will tell him . . .

BAINES: How—how you—?

LUAN: She will tell Husband because she wants to gain his favor.

BAINES: Why you tell me . . . all this thing?

LUAN: Reverend—when Chinese men convert to Christianity, what becomes of their many wives?

BAINES: Best idea: man choose, one woman be only true wife.

LUAN: And the rest of them?

BAINES: Can still live in house . . . but like—sisters, like—

LUAN: And the Christian man should have a Christian wife, yes?

BAINES: Yes, yes—this best thing.

LUAN: Well, then—will you be my advocate?

BAINES: "Advocate?"

LUAN: You understand. I think a lot more than you let on. I think we two can help each other—once you see how I can be of use to you in your work.

BAINES: You . . . help me?

LUAN: Husband says you have made few converts in many months. I can help you spread the word of Jesus—you see to it that I gain my rightful place.

BAINES: Yes?

LUAN: Reverend—the Chinese are a practical people. Let me arrange a great feast—for the entire village—at which the lord of the Great House pledges his allegiance to your God. You will be shocked how quickly the peasants rush to flatter my Husband by following in his footsteps. Like the good shepherd leading his flock. *(Pause)* And one more thing: when you preach, never ever say anything good about yourself—the less boastful you sound, the more you'll impress them. *(Pause)* Oh! Your cup is cold. I am the most terrible hostess this side of Australia. *(Luan pours tea)*

BAINES: You . . . you make Tieng-Bin . . . to leave room, no? So you and me . . . we talk, no? You make happen, no?

LUAN: Don't be ridiculous, Reverend. This is China. I nothing but woman and slave.

(Tieng-Bin enters with Ahn, the latter in too-large high-heeled pumps.)

Oh—look at her!

AHN: These are play shoes! They're too silly to wear in real life!

TIENG-BIN: But you don't seem so eager to take them off, do you?

AHN: They make me tall!—when I'm not falling over. Are you sure you do not want them, Auntie?

LUAN: I have told you many times, I cannot wear them.

AHN: Sorry. I forgot.

(Tieng-Bin crosses to Baines.)

TIENG-BIN: Forgive me, Reverend, for leaving you—

BAINES: No—no—

TIENG-BIN: But I have absolute confidence in the ability of Second Wife—

LUAN: Oh, please—

TIENG-BIN: —to keep things interesting.

LUAN: Our time together must have exposed me as a woman of very poor character. *(Pause)* Isn't that so, Reverend?

(Pause.)

BAINES: Your wife—she teach me so much, way of your people.

LUAN: The reverend flatters me—he must have Chinese blood. The truth is, we had a very significant encounter. Now, if you will both excuse me.

(Luan exits. Ahn practices walking with the heels.)

TIENG-BIN: I settle more disputes here each day than at work during the height of the trading season. See how it is, Reverend? With such duties, how can I possibly feel like an individual?

BAINES: Christian belief: each man, individual. But also, may I?

TIENG-BIN: Please, please.

BAINES: Prophet Paul say: each individual man have only one individual wife.

TIENG-BIN: Yes, I know that's the way of your people.

BAINES: He say, your body—body of God. No join body of God with dirty thing.

TIENG-BIN: Here in China, we say, whites are simply not man enough to handle more than one woman at a time.

BAINES: What *you* think?

TIENG-BIN: Reverend, there were times in Manila when I would see couples strolling arm in arm—thinking only of one another. And I would wonder . . . what it would be like to live a simpler life. *(Pause)* One wife? You whisper the idea as if it would offend me. When the truth is, Reverend, that it's a thought so precious, I whisper it, too.

BAINES: So, agree? One wife—who also love Jesus.

TIENG-BIN: It's not that simple. You haven't the faintest notion—

BAINES: This good, natural way of God.

TIENG-BIN: No, it's wrong; it's shameful; it's the way of destruction.

BAINES: Who say this?

TIENG-BIN: The ghosts at the altar. "The righteous man holds his First Wife forever in highest honor." "The position of wives is fixed, like the bodies of the heavens."

BAINES: This—evil voice.

TIENG-BIN: My parents, my ancestors? Reverend, I couldn't even remove Ahn's foot-bindings without hearing their voices. How could I take only one wife?

BAINES: Other missionary—they tell me about you.

TIENG-BIN: What do you mean?

BAINES: Tell me, "Master Eng—not like other lords. Others, when land fail, peasant starve, they shut their gate." Correct?

TIENG-BIN: It's none of my business what the other landowners—

BAINES: Please. Brag yourself. *(Pause)* You go Philippine, make money, save village. Other lords—they do this?

TIENG-BIN: No, not usually.

BAINES: Your own father—he do this?

TIENG-BIN: My father always tried to do the best he could.

BAINES: Before I come, already you not like other lords, not like father. Already you find new way. Must not fear to speak truth you know in your soul.

(Tieng-Bin moves toward his family altar. Lights slowly dim.)

TIENG-BIN: I am an individual.

BAINES: Good. Bible say, truth shall set you free.

TIENG-BIN: And I live in a new time, much different from that of my fathers.

BAINES: Yes, must be born again.

TIENG-BIN: I should be able to make my own way, live my own life, choose the woman I love.

BAINES: Prophet Paul say, "All I do mean nothing—if I no have love."

TIENG-BIN: To act out of love . . . to follow only the law of my own heart . . .

BAINES: Now, dead—no more power over you.

TIENG-BIN: Yes. The dead are just earth and dust and bones. (*He kneels before the altar*) Papa, Mama—you gave me life. But now I am a man. And you . . . You are dead.

(*Stage lights dim to separate spotlights on Baines and Ahn who stand apart.*)

BAINES (*British accent, perfect English*): "When I was a child, I spoke as a child, I thought as a child. But when I became a man, I put away childish things. For now we see as through a glass, darkly; but then shall we see face-to-face. And now abideth faith, hope, love, these three; but the greatest of these is love."

(*Lights cross-fade to Eling's pavilion. She lies in bed, nursing a swollen belly. Tieng-Bin enters, carrying a phonograph record.*)

TIENG-BIN: Italy can never be ignored, but the future—it comes from America.

ELING: What have you got there?

(*He unwraps a new 78, slips it onto the phonograph.*)

TIENG-BIN: This is a different kind of opera. Where men and women dance together dreaming they are anyone they wish to be.

(*He places the needle on the record. Scratchy recording of American dance music from the turn of the century.*)

May I have this dance? (*He takes her hands*) In the Philippines—I took lessons.

ELING: You must've been even lonelier than I thought.

TIENG-BIN: Come. I lead. You just follow. It's the way Western men show domination over their women.

(They dance together.)

ELING: I'll bet they didn't invent these steps for big, fat, pregnant cows with bound feet.

TIENG-BIN: Eling—the few extra inches are very erotic.

ELING: I'm swollen in places I never even knew existed. You wouldn't be like other lords, would you, and take a new wife, one who's slim and beautiful?

TIENG-BIN: Listen to the music. And try to imagine another world—better than this one. Where you . . . are my only wife.

ELING: You really held your teacher this close?

TIENG-BIN: Eling . . .

ELING: All right. My only Husband, shall we—shall we take my child up to the hills for a picnic this week?

TIENG-BIN: *Our* child. That sounds like an excellent idea.

ELING: Like a peasant family, but with money. Afterwards, we can all come here, to the American opera house.

TIENG-BIN: Except, our lives aren't only about our child. We're also two adults in love.

ELING: That's why we got married in the first place, right?

TIENG-BIN: And why we have no need—in fact, it would be impossible, illegal—for either of us to marry anyone else. *(Pause)* Eling—I think we can actually live such a life.

ELING: How? I think we would have to die and be reborn as new people.

TIENG-BIN: That's exactly right. Do you know what Reverend Baines and I have been discussing?

ELING: I'm not sure I—

TIENG-BIN: You. In a sense. He says I can pull down the family altars, live as though I had only one wife, even take you with me back to the Philippines. *(Eling pulls* *away from him)* Don't you like the idea? Can't you see, it's the best thing for you?

ELING: You want me to abandon my parents? Let their spirits wander alone for eternity? And if I went away with you, First Wife would lose such face. Is that what's best for us? To forget about others, and think only about ourselves?

TIENG-BIN: I thought you wanted to be modern.

ELING: I do. But does that mean I can no longer be Chinese?

(The record ends. Tieng-Bin removes the needle.)

TIENG-BIN: You know why this is so hard for you to understand? Because you've never even once attended Reverend Baines's lessons.

ELING: You said I didn't have to.

TIENG-BIN: But I—I thought you'd have *wanted* to come. Ahn took to the new teachings immediately.

ELING: So I hear.

TIENG-BIN: And Second Wife—

ELING: Don't start telling me about Luan.

TIENG-BIN: No, I really think even she's changing, becoming more generous—

ELING: Husband, how can you believe . . . ?

TIENG-BIN: What? *(Pause)* Eling?

ELING: Luan runs around behind your back telling anyone who'll listen that Ahn is only pretending to be interested in your religion so she can spy for First Wife.

(Tieng-Bin stares at Eling.)

TIENG-BIN: Ahn . . . has been lying to me? Ahn? First Wife put her up to this?

ELING: I'm sorry, Husband, but you're the only one who believes in this new religion. For the rest of us, nothing has changed.

TIENG-BIN: And you—you kept this hidden from me—for how long?

ELING: I didn't know what to—! It was none of my business. Second Wife should have told you herself.

TIENG-BIN: This isn't about Luan. You shouldn't have left me in the dark. I'll get to the bottom of this—

ELING: No! Please don't tell First Wife you heard this from me.

TIENG-BIN: This way of life—it brings out the worst in us all.

(Tieng-Bin exits.)

ELING: Husband! Please! Don't! *(To altar)* Papa, Mama—I only tried to tell the truth.

(Lights fade on Eling's pavilion, and come up on Siu-Yong's pavilion, revealing Ahn preparing opium for her mother's pipe. Siu-Yong lies on the floor in a drug-induced fog.)

TIENG-BIN *(Offstage)***:** First Wife—I am entering your pavilion!

(Siu-Yong rises unsteadily to her feet.)

SIU-YONG *(To Ahn)***:** Quickly—clear the air!

(Ahn scrambles to stash the drug paraphernalia, while Siu-Yong tries absurdly to blow the smoke clear. Tieng-Bin enters, causing Ahn to freeze in her tracks.)

Oh, Honored Husband. Please excuse the untidy state of my room. Had you given me proper notice, I would've had time to prepare refreshments.

TIENG-BIN: Ahn—now—out!

AHN: But . . .

TIENG-BIN: Now! *(Ahn moves toward the door, trying to conceal the opium pipe)* Ahn! *(Tieng-Bin snatches the pipe from her)*

(Ahn exits from the pavilion, but remains crouched outside in the shadows, listening.)

Opium, First Wife?

SIU-YONG: Really? Where?

TIENG-BIN: How can you even ask? When I'm holding the pipe in my hand, the air smelling like shit?

SIU-YONG: Not so hard. A good wife learns to disregard any number of facts. "See no evil, smell no evil."

TIENG-BIN: How could I have been home all this time and not even noticed?

SIU-YONG: A Husband is always the last to know. Servants are always the first, by the way.

TIENG-BIN: Have you been sending Ahn to spy on my lessons with Reverend Baines?

SIU-YONG: Who told you such a thing?

TIENG-BIN: That's not important.

SIU-YONG: How dare you—do you actually imagine I would ask our daughter to spy against her own father?

TIENG-BIN: Why don't we call Ahn back? And put the question to her directly?

SIU-YONG: On the other hand, it depends on your definition of a "spy."

TIENG-BIN: I see.

SIU-YONG: She was an innocent pawn.

TIENG-BIN: This is my home! You're not going to undermine my authority. We're going to have honest dealing here, is that clear?

SIU-YONG: What is this mania for honesty?

TIENG-BIN: Is everything a joke with you? Is nothing important?

SIU-YONG: Tieng-Bin! Don't leave me like this. We were promised to each other before we were born. *(Pause)* What is family anyway, but a loose collection of people with nothing in common but blood? Does blood cause all people to think alike? To love, or even like, one another? Of course not! If we wandered wherever our emotions might take us, we would all have murdered each other ages ago. That is why blood is not sufficient for order. Blood must be reinforced—by discipline. And your precious honesty is the mortal enemy of discipline. Confucius said: "In order to rule the nation, a man must first rule himself." So rule yourself! Tell me you haven't seen or heard anything tonight which would soil the honor of our family—and then have the discipline to believe your own words.

(*She lays back on her pillows*) Now—how about those refreshments?

TIENG-BIN: Siu-Yong, this woman you've become, I don't even know her.

SIU-YONG: If your answer is "no," then excuse me, I have my prayers to say before bed.

TIENG-BIN: You are my wife!

SIU-YONG: And I'm trying to behave like one.

TIENG-BIN: This home is going to be a model of change! No matter what you or your damn parents say.

SIU-YONG: I have never stood in the way of change. But tell me, Honored Husband, how much change can people endure?

TIENG-BIN: And this life is better? You shoving poison into your body? Second Wife telling secrets behind your back?

SIU-YONG: Second Wife? *She* said I'd made Ahn a spy? And you believed her?

(*Ahn leaves from outside the pavilion and exits the stage.*)

(*To altar*) Mama, Papa—do something.

TIENG-BIN: There you go again—worshipping your parents.

SIU-YONG: Yes, at least I pray to someone I know personally.

TIENG-BIN: Denounce them—or I'll force you to!

SIU-YONG: No! Papa, Mama—

TIENG-BIN: I said, stop it!

(Tieng-Bin throws Siu-Yong away from the altar.)

SIU-YONG: You—you order me around? Listen to yourself—scratch the surface, and you're still a traditional man. Deep inside, you want a traditional wife. You want me to remain as I am, admit it!

(Tieng-Bin positions himself between Siu-Yong and the altar.)

TIENG-BIN: I'm so traditional. All right—have it your way. *(He grabs the picture of Siu-Yong's parents)* What is it—that a traditional man does? Does he lose his temper? Does he order his wife around? Then punish her? Break her precious toys?
SIU-YONG: No! Don't!

(He smashes the picture. Siu-Yong screams.)

TIENG-BIN: When she disobeys him? When she blows smoke in the faces of his children? Is this the sort of thing he does?

(He leaves the picture in a heap on the ground and stands back.)

I have made my decision. Or you've made it for me. I *will* be baptized. And all the family altars will come down at once. *(Pause)* The servants will search for any more of the drug you may have hidden. Then—you'll start attending Pastor Baines's lessons. We all need a fresh start, to begin a new life.

(Siu-Yong remains on the floor. Tieng-Bin exits. Siu-Yong crawls to the rubble of her parents' portrait. She cradles it in her arms.)

SIU-YONG (*To portrait*): Papa, Mama—what terrible things did you do, that my life should go so wrong?

(*Lights fade on Siu-Yong's pavilion and come up on Luan's. Luan opens her eyes and sees Ahn looking down on her. She is startled.*)

LUAN: Huh? Ahn, you scared me! Idiot—have you added sleepwalking to your list of defects?

AHN: I am a Golden Child.

LUAN: "Golden Child, Golden Child."

AHN: And for your schemes against First Wife, you must now eat bitter.

LUAN: You know what Westerners say is golden? Silence. Now give me that lantern.

(*Ahn snatches the lantern up before Luan can reach it.*)

AHN: Your grandmother, I hear her voice. And she says: "Unworthy granddaughter, how dare you betray your sacred duties to those who gave you life."

LUAN: This is the height of—

(*Luan reaches for the lantern. Ahn slaps her face.*)

AHN: "Wicked granddaughter—" (*Ahn slaps her again*) "You can't spit in the face of the dead without eating the bitter fruit."

LUAN: Now give me that—

(*Ahn pushes her down to the floor.*)

AHN: "How dare you strike your grandmother."

LUAN: You're . . . not my . . .

AHN: "Hear our voices. We starve because you do not feed us."

LUAN: Ah Ying!

AHN: "You scheme with the foreigners to turn our family against us."

LUAN: Isn't anyone on duty here?

AHN: "As you abandoned your ancestors, so your children will abandon you after your death."

LUAN: Yung-Bin, Yung-Bin would never—

AHN: "Your son will grow ashamed of you, and future generations will not even remember your name."

LUAN: Yung-Bin will rule this family. I will live to see the day.

AHN: "No, your son will curse the day you told Husband that First Wife sent a spy against him—"

LUAN: What?

AHN: "For on that day, his fortune—"

LUAN: Wait one second. I didn't.

AHN: "His fortune was lost; his anchor tether to the shore was—"

LUAN: If someone told Husband about your little assignment, it certainly wasn't me. *(Pause)* What kind of ghosts get their facts wrong, huh?

AHN: You lie—you always lie.

LUAN: I'll tell you what kind—false ghosts—who speak from the mouth of a peasant girl, whose skin reeks of opium, who calls herself a Golden Child while, deep inside, even she knows she's an ugly little liar. *(She snatches the light away from Ahn)* Ghosts have no more power over me. I'm a Christian now! So—would you like to hear *me* tell the future? I'm the only one who's been right up to this point. *(Draws back to hit Ahn, ends up patting her on the cheek instead)* Jesus saves. He will save me and destroy your mother. He will take our miserable lives, all the injustice within these walls, and make everything born again. *(Pause)* Thank you for letting me know what happened tonight. It won't be long now before I'm First Wife—in fact, if not in name. Take my advice, Ahn—join us, forget your mother—and save yourself. Or else be washed away like the peasants in the flood.

(Ahn exits. Lights fade on Luan's pavilion. Reverend Baines enters and crosses to baptism font.)

BAINES: Resident of city of Eng . . . so good, see so many of you gather today, for great feast, wondrous fine festivity! One hundred thousand thanks to lord of the great house, Master Eng! Who give unworthy self great fortune, meet all you honorable friends. *(Pause)* I—idiot man. My mother should have drown me in well before I learn to speak. Anyone say I smart, they no have brain. But Master Eng teach me so much, China way. Now, if any you visit ugly mission, hear my bad Chinese, I hope perhaps you find I am . . . tiny little bit not so stupid. *(Pause)* Now—wondrous miracle: Master Eng family— choose here, today—receive baptism, make holy water, swallow Jesus body fluid.

(Split scene: as Baines administers the sacrament of baptism, lights come up on Siu-Yong in her pavilion with Ahn. Siu-Yong produces three balls of opium hidden in her altar.)

I call Eng Tieng-Bin.

(Tieng-Bin enters, in Western suit.)

"Eng Tieng-Bin, you desire, be baptized?"
TIENG-BIN: "I do, by the grace of God."
BAINES: "You renounce Satan?"
TIENG-BIN: "I renounce Satan and all the spiritual forces of wickedness that rebel against God."
BAINES: "You renounce sin?"
TIENG-BIN: "I renounce all sinful desires that draw me from the love of God."
BAINES: "Eng Tieng-Bin, you are seal by holy spirit baptism, mark as Christ's own, forever."

(Baines makes sign of the cross on Tieng-Bin's forehead and feeds him wafer and wine.)

SIU-YONG *(To Ahn)*: "The servants will search for your opium." So pathetic. Who does your father think the servants work for? To hand me over to the missionary butchers—you must learn to put your foot down, Daughter. Such behavior is unacceptable, we mustn't allow it.

AHN: Mama . . . don't eat that.

SIU-YONG: Duty calls.

(Siu-Yong puts the first ball into her mouth, swallows it.)

BAINES: I call Eng Luan, receive the baptism. "Eng Luan, you desire, be baptized?"

LUAN: "I do, by the grace of God."

BAINES: "You renounce evil?"

LUAN: "I renounce the evil powers of this world which corrupt and destroy the creatures of God."

(Baines makes sign of cross on Luan's forehead and feeds her wafer and wine.)

BAINES: "Eng Luan, you are seal by Holy Spirit baptism, mark as Christ's own, forever."

SIU-YONG *(To Ahn)*: You will smile at the reverend, perhaps even kiss the Christian idol—but I know you will also worship and provide for me—in secret, where all the important things in this world happen.

(Siu-Yong eats the second ball of opium.)

BAINES: I call Eng Eling, receive the baptism. "Eng Eling, you desire, be baptized?"

ELING: "I do."

BAINES: "You believe in Jesus Christ, accept him as savior?"
ELING: "I do."

(Baines makes sign of cross on Eling's forehead and feeds her wafer and wine.)

BAINES: "Eng Eling, you are seal by Holy Spirit baptism, mark as Christ's own, forever. Amen."

(Baines blesses them.)

SIU-YONG: And you will succeed because you know the central lesson of life: that humility is power. And death is the ultimate humility.

(Siu-Yong eats the third ball.)

BAINES: "We accept you into house of God. Amen."
BAINES, TIENG-BIN, LUAN AND ELING: "Amen."

(Baines, Eling, Tieng-Bin and Luan exit.)

SIU-YONG: Now come here. And let me sing you to sleep.

(Siu-Yong takes Ahn in her arms, and rocks her while singing a lullaby:)

A brother and sister
As drought hit far and wide
They saw their parents starving
As crops around them died
These dutiful sweet children
Knew just what to do
From pieces of their own flesh
Made Mom and Dad a stew
To serve your parents
Is life's most precious goal

And if you're very lucky
They'll one day eat you whole
With a hi diddle dee
The soup gets sister's nose
And a ho ho ho . . .

(Siu-Yong loses consciousness.)

AHN: Ma? Ma?

(Ahn runs offstage. Fade to black.
Lights up on Eling's pavilion. Christian hymns are playing on her phonograph. She kneels before her family altar, her parents' portrait now replaced by a crucifix. Her belly is large in the final stages of pregnancy.)

ELING: "The lord is my shepherd, I shall not want." *(To altar)* Papa, Mama—I have to do this for my Husband. He saved not only me, but all your children, from poverty and hunger. *(Pause)* "He leadeth me beside the still waters . . ." *(Pause)* But if you see First Wife up there—

(Siu-Yong's voice is heard over the house speakers.)

SIU-YONG'S VOICE: Three tips for a well-ordered household.
ELING: Tell her, please—
SIU-YONG'S VOICE: One, the less you know about your relatives, the easier it is to love them.
ELING: Don't be angry at me, I didn't mean to tell him—
SIU-YONG'S VOICE: Two, never betray weakness in the home, it only encourages them.
ELING: I just couldn't let Husband fool himself like that.
SIU-YONG'S VOICE: And three, if, as happens in even the best families, a relative should cause your death—
ELING: Ask her to forgive me. As her sister? Bound by true affection?

SIU-YONG'S VOICE: —don't forget to return to take your revenge.

(*Siu-Yong bursts into Eling's pavilion. She wears ghost robes. Hymns cross-fade to Chinese opera music.*)

ELING: Older Sister! I—

SIU-YONG: You learned your lessons in womanhood a little too well, I'm afraid.

ELING: No, I didn't learn a thing. I'm a fool, simple-minded, an idiot—

SIU-YONG: Quiet! You have some nerve, complimenting yourself at a time like this.

ELING: But—

SIU-YONG: Once, I actually believed you were stupid.

ELING: But I am! I must be the stupidest wife in all China!

SIU-YONG: Or the most clever. The other ghosts couldn't wait to reveal that it was you who betrayed me to Husband. It seems I grossly underestimated you.

ELING: No, I'm a good person, a humble servant, a dutiful daughter—

SIU-YONG: Dutiful?—Oh, please.

ELING: What do you know?

SIU-YONG: You forget—I'm dead. I've seen your parents.

ELING: No, you don't know them—

SIU-YONG: Now that you have stopped providing for them—

ELING: My brothers and sisters, they must be—

SIU-YONG: What can they do but sell themselves as slaves?

ELING: Slaves?

SIU-YONG: Now they work for your former neighbors, the Wongs.

ELING: Not the Wongs! The Wongs were evil people! What are they doing up there? They should be sent to hell!

SIU-YONG: Maybe that's true, but *they* have dutiful children. How many times do I have to tell you: life is not personal!

(*Eling runs for the door.*)

ELING: I'll call Reverend Baines—he'll send you away.

SIU-YONG: With his Chinese? I wouldn't even be able to understand his exorcism. No, the only people who can protect you from a ghost are your ancestors.

ELING: I'll pray for them. I'll burn offerings, somehow . . .

SIU-YONG: What if Husband should find out? He'd be so disappointed. In his old-fashioned wife.

ELING: I have to be a modern person. Just like Husband. And Second Wife. And even Ahn.

SIU-YONG: Maybe *they* are. But you will never be. (*Pause*) Some people were not created for change. Their minds are not large enough, their souls insufficiently ruthless. These are the people left behind, their names forgotten, as time rolls on. I should know. Look into my eyes—and see yourself.

(*Eling falls to her knees before the crucifix and flings it aside. She lights the candle for burning offerings. Siu-Yong moves behind Eling.*)

ELING (*To altar*): Papa, Mama, I don't know what to do.

SIU-YONG: You know you're not fit to live in Husband's new world.

ELING: I can't let you starve, but I can't disobey my Husband either.

SIU-YONG: He'll take you to the Philippines; you won't know how to live there—with each passing day, he'll grow more ashamed of you.

ELING: No, I can't let that happen.

SIU-YONG: You are not the woman he thinks you are.

ELING: Maybe I'm not. But I love him.

SIU-YONG: Love! You don't know the meaning of love! You're grateful, that is all.

ELING: Sometimes, I wish I'd never even come to this house!

SIU-YONG: Then perhaps it is time for you to leave.

(*Siu-Yong waves her ghost sleeves. Eling cries out as the pains of labor begin.*)

ELING: All these demands—how can I live up to them?

SIU-YONG: There is a way. To serve your parents, to serve your Husband.

ELING: How? Please, Older Sister—help me.

SIU-YONG: Come with me. You are needed elsewhere—with your parents.

(Siu-Yong shakes sleeves. Eling feels another contraction.)

ELING: But . . . what about my baby?

SIU-YONG: Your old thinking will only spoil his future.

(Siu-Yong leads Eling to the bed.)

ELING: Yes, you're right. It's time to prove . . . that I *can* sacrifice for others. This is the best thing for Husband.

SIU-YONG: It is best for your Husband, it is best for your parents, it is best for your child. And to a good Chinese woman, what else could possibly matter?

(Siu-Yong shakes sleeves. Eling screams in labor. Ahn enters, runs to Eling.)

AHN *(Calling off)*: Papa!

(Tieng-Bin, Baines and Luan enter, and cross to Eling's bed. Hidden, Eling rolls off the back of the bed, and crosses to Siu-Yong. Siu-Yong places ghost robes on Eling and leads her into the spirit world. Baines, Luan and Ahn exit, leaving Tieng-Bin alone in Eling's pavilion.)

TIENG-BIN: Eling? Eling. *(Tieng-Bin collapses at Eling's altar. He burns offerings with increasing speed and recklessness)* How can I make you understand that I did it all for you? You must take everything now—everything with you— all my ideals, my memories of the world, my experience with far-off peoples—all the rooms I've filled to bursting with empty words—words of change, of progress—all the rooms where I had hidden our future. (*Eling's pavilion is catching on fire*) Papa, Mama—this is how you punish a disobedient son? Take from me the wife I love, even the wife I respect, leaving me with the one for whom I feel . . . nothing. I don't give a damn anymore about the living or the dead. Yes, by embracing the West, I have finally become . . . an individual.

(*Ahn enters.*)

AHN: All right, Papa. That's enough. Come out before you set the whole pavilion on fire.

TIENG-BIN: I can do whatever I want. Leave me alone!

AHN: "God will not test us beyond what we can bear."

TIENG-BIN: What kind of nonsense are you—?

AHN: I listened to the words of the preacher, remember? Now, rise up and walk!

TIENG-BIN: You can't talk that way to me—you are only my daughter!

AHN: That is the old way. The Bible says—

TIENG-BIN: I don't want to hear another word about this God.

AHN: "All things work together for good—"

TIENG-BIN: Get out!

AHN: "—for those that love the Lord."

TIENG-BIN: Shut your mouth! (*Tieng-Bin strikes Ahn, then pulls away, shocked. She stands her ground*) Ahn—I didn't mean to—

AHN: Papa—you can hit me, but you can't make me go away. I'm not a little girl anymore.

TIENG-BIN: I should've listened to your mother.

AHN: No—she was wrong, Papa. (*Pause*) Mama believed in our ancestors; she did everything for them. But when she called on them for help, there was nothing they could do. I watched her eat opium and die. So I'm not going to believe in them anymore. I can't end up like her. I'm going to follow this new God, the one you brought into our home. Papa, we must all be born again.

TIENG-BIN: What have I done to you all?

(She leads him out of the pavilion.)

AHN: You've thought enough for one life. It's time to let your children take over. So get up. The servants will be coming. I don't care how badly you feel; we don't try to kill ourselves in front of the help.

(Luan enters.)

LUAN: Husband, such a tragedy! We must say a prayer for Eling and the child that was lost.

TIENG-BIN: Will you leave us, Second Wife?

LUAN: Oh, slip of the tongue—my only Husband.

TIENG-BIN: Will you leave us alone . . . my only wife?

LUAN: Whatever you desire. *(Calling off)* Ah Ying! Ah Ying!

(Luan exits.)

TIENG-BIN: I don't know . . . how to go on from here.

AHN: You must go back to the Philippines. If the business fails, who cares what God we worship?

TIENG-BIN: Daughter—someday, when you are all grown, you will look back and hate me—for what I did to your mother.

AHN: Impossible, Papa. When my children ask about our family, I'll tell great stories about you—how you made us all born again. But First Wife, I will not—no, I swear, I will not even remember her name.

(Ahn begins to cry.)

TIENG-BIN: Ahn, your mother was from another time, that's all. I will always honor her name.

AHN: And I will always be grateful to you, Papa—even when I am old, even after I die.

TIENG-BIN: How can you possibly know such things?

AHN: Because I am a Golden Child.

(Lights and set transform. Tieng-Bin becomes Andrew; Ahn becomes an old woman again.)

When season change, we leave forever, home of our ancestor. Your grandfather, after this, he does not live so long. Few years later, Second Wife send me far away, to new land, call "America."

ANDREW: You see? Why I don't want to become a parent? Your father tried so hard, but he only brought tragedy to himself and everyone around him.

AHN: No. He suffer to bring family into future. Where better life, I am able to live. I first girl in family go school, choose own husband—and all the time, worship Jesus.

ANDREW: So—whenever you opened a Bible, or said a prayer to Jesus, you were actually making an offering . . . to your father. In spite of everything, you loved him so much.

AHN: My father, Tieng-Bin—this one thing I will never forget: you see, he is the one . . . who take the binding from my feet.

(In bed, Elizabeth stirs. Andrew sees her.)

ANDREW: Eling?

ELIZABETH *(Waking)*: Who's Eling?

ANDREW: Sorry. I was just remembering a story my mother used to tell me. About my grandfather.

ELIZABETH: You never told me about your grandfather.

ANDREW: He wanted to start a new family with the woman he loved. And to make that happen, he tried to move heaven and earth.

AHN: Andrew—write it down.

ANDREW: You know, I think I'll write it down.

ELIZABETH: You never write about your family.

ANDREW: I want to preserve this. For our child. Like my mother did for me.

ELIZABETH: Maybe you should talk to your mother more often.

ANDREW: Maybe I will.

AHN: Next—you must buy nice house in suburb.

ELIZABETH: Andrew, I'm really looking forward to watching our baby grow up. And you, too. Now try and get some sleep.

(She kisses him, goes to sleep. As he speaks, First Wife and Second Wife appear.)

ANDREW: I watch your mother sleeping, knowing you are growing inside her. And suddenly the room is filled with spirits—so many faces, looking down on me. And on each face, a story, some I have been told, some I can only imagine, and some I will never know at all. But many of them, people not so different from myself, who struggled with what to keep, and what to change—for the next generation. And I realize my face too will one day join this constellation. Perhaps, if I do my best, in the imagination of my descendants, I may also one day be born again. I feel the eyes of our ancestors upon us, all awaiting together the birth of you, my Golden Child.

(Elizabeth rolls over and holds him. First Wife, Second Wife and Ahn sit on their bed. Lights fade to black.)

END OF PLAY